Shine Like a UNICORN

BY Shelli R. Johannes

ILLUSTRATED BY Maddie Frost

HARPER
An Imprint of HarperCollinsPublishers

To Madelyn and Gray, for not being afraid to stand out
as unicorns in a herd of horses
—S.J.

For my magical mother
—M.F.

Shine Like a Unicorn
Text copyright © 2021 by Shelli R. Johannes
Illustrations copyright © 2021 by Maddie Frost

ISBN 978-0-06-299833-0

The artist used Adobe Photoshop to create the digital illustrations for this book.
Book Design by Marisa Rother
21 22 23 24 25   RTLO   10 9 8 7 6 5 4 3 2 1
❖
First Edition

Do you want to shine like a unicorn?

Of course you do!
After all, unicorns are special.
Totally **uni-que.** (Get it?)

It's not easy being a unicorn.

Many have tried.

A for effort.

But if you **REALLY** want to be a unicorn, follow these secret steps.

STEP 1:
Choose a unicorn name.

Unicorns love to have crazy names.
Pick a fun word and add a silly adjective.

Prancing Sparkles and Happy Sunshine are popular.
Lucky Charm is so on trend.

My name is **Glitter Poop.**
I know it's different,
but that's the point!

STEP 2: stand out in a herd.

Unicorns show off our own style.
Sometimes that means experimenting with color.

Or hats.
The bigger, the better.

You can always find me in a crowd.

STEP 3: Be curious!

Unicorns love to ask questions.
Why? Excellent question!
(See? You would be a great unicorn!)
Because being smart is cool!

I especially love to learn big words. Sometimes I can be grandiloquent, which leaves others gobsmacked.

Impressive, right?

STEP 4: Find your fun.

Unicorns love to horse around.
If we get bored, we make up new games.
Hockey dancing and ribbon skating are so fun.

Horn pop is a blast!

I invented donut holes . . .
so we can eat and play
at the same time.

BRILLIANT!

STEP 5: Mind your manners.

Unicorns are very polite.

We say "please" and "thank you."
Normally.

We hold doors open for others.
Usually.

And we love to share.
Mostly.

Though patience is not
always our virtue.

Sometimes I make mistakes.

Hey, at least I'm polite about it.

Now for **STEP 6 . . .**

WAIT.

What did you say?
You already do all these steps?

Well, then you are on your way
to being totally **uni-tastic!**

However, I'm just getting started.

STEP 6: Search for the bright side.

Unicorns work hard to be happy.

It's not always easy.

We can be grumpy too.

If we get mad, we aren't afraid
to kick off some steam.

Sometimes I cry—
because it's okay to be sad.

But I try to look for rainbows,
even on extra cloudy days.

Look,
there's one now.

STEP 7: Love yourself.

Unicorns know we're not perfect.
And that's okay.

Even we have
crazy hair days.

Sometimes we have
upside-down days where
nothing looks right.

Other times, we question ourselves:

"Is my horn too short?"
"Is my tail too long?"
"Is my rump too glittery?"

Because I can't tell.

But, then we remember that . . . imperfections make us **flawsome!**

STEP 8:
Dream extra BIG.

Unicorns keep our hooves on the ground . . .

. . . and our heads in the clouds.

But beware, too much daydreaming can cause dream freeze.

That's when a unicorn has big dreams about where he's going but forgets where he is.

Wait, you do all that too?
Well, then hold on to your **uni-horns!**
Because there is only one more step.

The MOST IMPORTANT UNICORNY step of all. **STEP 9!**

Why 9? Excellent question! (Refer to Step 3.)
Because unicorns love surprises.

Don't turn the page
unless you are ready
for the last step!

WARNING:
YOU CANNOT BE A UNICORN WITHOUT STEP 9.

DISCLAIMER:
IF YOU TURN THE PAGE, YOU MAY NEVER SEE UNICORNS THE SAME WAY AGAIN!

I think you get the point.

STEP 9:
We make our own magic!

Even though unicorns don't have fairy dust
and can't fly, we sure can have fun trying!

Now hold your pointer finger up to your forehead.
And yell the Unicorn Motto after me:

U DO U!

CONGRATULATIONS!

You are now an official unicorn!

Now go shine. Just like me!